Barbara Diamond Goldin

The Best Hanukkah Ever

Illustrated by Avi Katz

Marshall Cavendish Children

Marshall Cavendish Corporation, 99 White Plains Road, Tarrytown, NY 10591
www.marshallcavendish.us/kids

Library of Congress Cataloging-in-Publication Data
Goldin, Barbara Diamond.
The Best Hanukkah ever / by Barbara Diamond Goldin ; illustrated by Avi Katz. — 1st ed.
p. cm.
Summary: When the Knoodle family tries to follow their rabbi's advice about giving the perfect gift,
everything goes wrong and their Hanukkah seems ruined until the rabbi comes to straighten things out.
ISBN 978-0-7614-5355-0
[1. Gifts—Fiction. 2. Hanukkah—Fiction. 3. Jews—United States—Fiction. 4. Family life—Fiction.] I. Katz, Avi, ill. II. Title.
PZ7.G5674Bes 2007
[E]—dc22
2006030235

The text of this book is set in Cochin.
The illustrations are rendered in digital media.

Book design by Vera Soki
Editor: Margery Cuyler

Printed in China
First edition
1 3 5 6 4 2

In memory of my beloved father, Morton Diamond
— Barbara Diamond Goldin

For Rachel with love
— Avi Katz

It was the Saturday night before Hanukkah, and the Knoodle family was sitting around the kitchen table eating their supper.

"Did you hear what the rabbi said in synagogue this morning?" asked Papa Jack.

Mama Pearl finished the last spoonful of her chicken soup.

"Such a smart rabbi," she said. "He told us, 'It is hard to give the perfect gift, one that will be treasured forever.'"

The Knoodles silently pondered the rabbi's words. Bubby Sadie thought so much that her nose wrinkled. Mama Pearl got a headache. Little Yekl tumbled off his chair.

The family vowed to practice the rabbi's
wise advice.

Papa Jack put everyone's name in a hat.
Each Knoodle was to give a gift to the
person whose name was picked.

On the first night of Hanukkah, the family lit the menorah, sang holiday songs, and told the Hanukkah story. The smell of Mama Pearl's potato pancakes filled the air. So did the Knoodles' laughing and shrieking each time they spun the dreidel.

Then it came time to exchange the presents. The Knoodles pulled out their perfect gifts.

"Such a pile I never saw!" said Papa Jack.

"Youngest goes first," said Mama Pearl.

The gift for Little Yekl was as round and big as Little Yekl himself. He thumped on the package. It made a hollow sound. Bubby Sadie smiled proudly. "It's from me," she said. Little Yekl tore off the paper.

"Why, Bubby Sadie!" exclaimed Mama Pearl. "It's a pickle barrel! Just like Grandma Alte's in the Old Country!"

"Such pickles she made!" Bubby Sadie licked her lips. "It kills me to give that old barrel away. But like the rabbi said, 'It is hard to give the perfect gift.'"

Little Yekl started banging the wooden barrel like a drum.

Bubby Sadie frowned. "Such a nice pickle barrel and see what he does!"

"Don't fuss," Mama Pearl said. "He'll enjoy his pickle barrel when he's older."

"Open my present, Papa Jack," said Mama.

Papa Jack unwrapped his present and held it in his hands—a straw hat with yellow daisies circling the brim and purple ribbons cascading down the back.

Papa Jack didn't say a word.

"I've wanted a hat like that my whole life," said Mama Pearl.

Papa Jack sat quietly. "I know what I'll do!"
He grabbed his motorcycle helmet from the
hat tree and plunked the straw hat on top of it.
"I'll start a new style," said Papa Jack.

Mama Pearl stamped her foot. "You'll stretch it out of shape," she said crossly.

"Ach! These Knoodle husbands!" said Bubby Sadie. "What do they know of hats!"

Papa Jack handed Mama Pearl her present. "Look what I got you," he said. "It'll put a smile back on your face. A Knoodle guarantee!"

Mama Pearl pulled off the paper and saw a sparkly red guitar.

"I can't play this!" she snapped.

"Then learn," said Papa Jack, looking wistfully at the lovely guitar. "I wish somebody had given one to me."

"Open my present, Bubby Sadie," Shayna said.
"A curling iron!" Bubby Sadie wailed. "If only I had
more hair left to curl." She began to sob.

All at once, Shayna's present jumped.
    She fell backward. "What kind of present jumps?"
she asked.

"Tree frogs!" cried Little Yekl. "They're beauties, too.
I've been visiting them at the pet shop every day after school."
Shayna screamed.

Papa Jack went redder than a beet.

Mama Pearl glared at the helmet, with her hat smashed down over it.

Bubby Sadie sadly stroked the few hairs left on her head and cried louder.

Little Yekl stomped and thumped his pickle barrel, making the house shake with the horrible racket. The Knoodles were miserable. This was their worst Hanukkah ever.

"Jack, go get the rabbi!" ordered
Bubby Sadie.
"On Hanukkah?" said Papa Jack.
But soon he was back with the rabbi.

Mama Pearl was the first to complain. "We did just what you said. We gave one another a perfect gift, but none of us is happy."

Bubby Sadie shook her finger at the rabbi. "See what happened because of you!"

The rabbi looked at the angry Knoodles.
"This is a big mistake. I said, 'It's hard to give the perfect gift, one that will be treasured forever.'

That means it should be a treasure to who gets it, not to who gives it!"

"Well, what will we do now?" cried Bubby Sadie. "Our Hanukkah is ruined!"

Little Yekl jumped up. "No, it isn't!" he shouted.

He rolled the pickle barrel to Bubby Sadie,
who affectionately pinched his cheek.

Papa Jack peeled the hat off his motorcycle helmet and tied it onto Mama Pearl's head. She kissed her husband and presented him with the shiny guitar.

Shayna caught the frogs and gave them to Little Yekl.

Bubby Sadie picked up the curling iron and gave it to Shayna.

"Just what I always wanted!" beamed Mama Pearl.

"Me, too! Me, too!" all the Knoodles yelled at once. They grabbed hands and did a little dance around the rabbi.

"This is the best Hanukkah ever," said Shayna.
"We are one smart family," crowed Little Yekl.

"That's a Knoodle for you," said Papa Jack.